#1
KRAYON

THE ILLUSTRATIONS IN THIS BOOK WERE MADE IN
ADOBE PHOTOSHOP AND WITH 100% FEARLESSNESS.

CATALOGING-IN-PUBLICATION DATA HAS BEEN APPLIED FOR
AND MAY BE OBTAINED FROM THE LIBRARY OF CONGRESS.
ISBN: 978-1-4197-0379-9

BOOK DESIGN BY DAN SANTAT AND CHAD W. BECKERMAN

PUBLISHED IN 2012 BY ABRAMS BOOKS FOR YOUNG READERS,
AN IMPRINT OF ABRAMS.

PRINTED AND BOUND IN CHINA
10 9 8 7 6 5 4 3 2

ABRAMS
THE ART OF BOOKS SINCE 1949
115 WEST 18TH STREET
NEW YORK, NY 10011
WWW.ABRAMSBOOKS.COM

TO BRYAN AND ANN GILLIGAN
AND THEIR FEARLESS SON, KELLAN.
-M.B.

FOR LEAH, ALEK, AND KYLE.
-D.S.

KEL GILLIGAN'S DAREDEVIL STUNT SHOW

ABRAMS BOOKS FOR YOUNG READERS, NEW YORK

written by
MICHAEL
BUCKLEY

I'M KEL GILLIGAN AND I'M A DAREDEVIL! I PERFORM SUPER SCARY STUNTS WHILE LAUGHING IN THE FACE OF DANGER.
THEY CALL ME "THE BOY WITHOUT FEAR."
AUXIER

WHAT? YOU'VE NEVER HEARD OF ME?
REALLY?
THEN YOU'VE NEVER HEARD ABOUT THE TIME I PUT MY LIFE AT RISK EATING . . .

1:03:07:43

BROCCOLI

NEW FOODS ARE HORRIFYING!

PLEASE STOP!

84min

1:03:08:16
CHEW
CHEW
CHEW
83 min

1:03:08:36

HE HAS SOME KIND OF DEATH WISH!

HAS HE LOST HIS MIND?

83 min

IT WAS CLOSE, BUT I WALKED AWAY WITHOUT A SCRATCH ON ME.

THAT ONE MADE THE TEN O'CLOCK NEWS. IF YOU HAVEN'T HEARD ABOUT THAT STUNT, THEN YOU'VE PROBABLY NEVER HEARD ABOUT THE TIME I THREW CAUTION TO THE WIND AND FACED . . .

THE POTTY OF DOOM!
DUN-DUN-DUHHHHH!
164min

0:02:49:08

THAT STUNT TOOK A LITTLE LONGER THAN I EXPECTED.

I SHOULD HAVE BROUGHT A COLORING BOOK OR SOMETHING.

0:04:13:06

TA-DAAA!

He's AMAZING!

82min

BIG KID STUFF CAN BE TERRIFYING, BUT I LAUGH AT TERROR. HA!

WELL, I'M BACK WITH ALL NEW DEEDS OF DERRING-DO, SO IF YOU ARE EASILY SPOOKED, I SUGGEST YOU LOOK AWAY.

FOR MY FIRST STUNT OF THE DAY . . .

I'M GOING TO GET DRESSED ALL BY MYSELF!
WITHOUT A NET?
HE'S CRAZY!

OOOFFF!
UNHHH!
AIEEEEE!
UGGGHHH!
DON'T WORRY, FOLKS.
I KNOW WHAT I'M DOING.

TA-DAAA!
AHHHHHHH!

LET'S MOVE ON. THIS IS MY MOM.
SHE'S TALKING ON THE PHONE.
WHICH MEANS SHE'S NOT TALKING TO ME!
FOR MY NEXT ACT I WILL ATTEMPT TO
KEEP MYSELF BUSY WHILE SHE
FINISHES HER CONVERSATION . . .

UNINTERRUPTED!!
THAT'S IMPOSSIBLE!
IT CAN'T BE DONE!

DON'T PANIC! I KNOW THAT MOM WILL SOON HANG UP THE PHONE.

I SAID, I KNOW SHE WILL SOON HANG UP THE PHONE!!!

TA-DAAAAA!!!
CLICK
IF I HADN'T SEEN IT, I WOULDN'T HAVE BELIEVED IT!!
CLAP *CLAP* *CLAP*

MY NEXT HEART-RACING STUNT WILL TEST MY NERVES UNDERWATER. YES, IT'S . . .

BATH TIME!!!

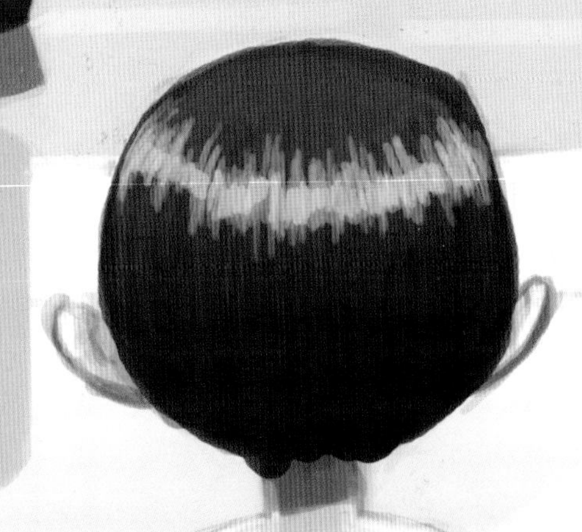

I'M RISKING LIFE AND LIMB BY TAKING A BATH WITH ONE ASSISTANT. BUT I'M KEL GILLIGAN!
DADDY, LET'S DO THIS!

SCRUB
SCRUB
SCRUB

SPLASH!

SQUEAK
SQUEAK
SQUEAK

HA HA
HA
HA
HA
HA HA
HA
HA
HA

TA-DAAA!!!
HE KNOWS NO FEAR!

IT'S TIME FOR MY LAST STUNT, AND I SUGGEST YOU SIT DOWN FOR THIS, BECAUSE I'M GOING TO GO TO BED . . .
WITHOUT CHECKING THE ROOM FOR MONSTERS! GO AHEAD AND SHUT OFF THE LIGHT!
GASP!
CLAP CLAP CLAP

I CAN'T LOOK!

I'M NOT AFRAID AT ALL . . .

THUMP!

. . . MONSTERS ARE SILLY . . .

THUMP! THUMP!

MOMMY!

DADDY!

SOME STUNTS ARE BEST LEFT TO THE PROFESSIONALS.

FOR MY LAST STUNT I'M GOING TO KEEP MY PARENTS SAFE FROM MONSTERS UNDER *THEIR* BED. DON'T WORRY, MOM AND DAD—THERE'S NOTHING TO BE AFRAID OF. I DO DANGEROUS STUFF LIKE THIS ALL THE TIME.

I
DANGER

THE END